EAGLE DRUM

ROBERT CRUM

FOUR WINDS PRESS ⚡ maxwell macmillan canada toronto maxwell macmillan international new york oxford singapore sydney

EAGLE DRUM

on the powwow trail with a young grass dancer

for my parents,
Robert and Betty Crum

A NOTE FROM THE AUTHOR

Louis Pierre and his grandfather, Pat, are members of the Pend Oreille tribe (pronounced *pond a-ray*). The Pend Oreilles are the original inhabitants of the Mission Valley in western Montana. With the signing of the Hellgate Treaty in 1855, the Pend Oreille, Salish, and Kootenai tribes ceded most of western Montana to the United States, reserving the area west of the Mission Mountains for themselves. Today the reservation, called the Flathead Reservation (Flathead is the name given to the tribes associated with the region), is managed as a political confederation of all three tribes.

Most of the photographs in this book were taken at the United Peoples Powwow (Missoula, Mont.) and the Annual Spokane Tribal Fair & Rodeo (Wellpinit, Wash.) in the summer of 1992. Additional photographs were taken at the Crow Fair & Rodeo (Crow Agency, Mont.), Arlee Powwow & Celebration (Arlee, Mont.), and the First Peoples Powwow (St. Augustine, Fla.).

ACKNOWLEDGMENTS

The author would like to express his appreciation to Louis, Pat, Michael, and David Pierre, along with the rest of their family, for their help and generosity. Thanks also to Dallas Chief Eagle, Jr., for contributing the introduction, and to Joe Whitehawk for reading and checking the manuscript, and to the good people of the Flathead Reservation in Montana.

Library of Congress Cataloging-in-Publication Data   Crum, Robert. Eagle drum : on the powwow trail with a young grass dancer / by Robert Crum.—1st ed.   p.   cm. ISBN 0-02-725515-8 1.Kalispel Indians—Juvenile literature. 2. Pierre, Louis—Juvenile literature. 3. Powwows—Juvenile literature. 4. Indians of North America—Dances—Juvenile literature. I. Title. E99.K17C77 1994 394´.3—dc20 94-6034

ST. IGNATIUS

INTRODUCTION

The *Wacipi*, which is the Lakota Indian word for "powwow dance," is the oldest ceremony in America and probably one of the most basic. It unites us to the earth. It reaches back to the time when the two-leggeds, four-leggeds, and rooted beings were all one family. When we dance, stepping lightly with our feet on the earth, wearing our outfits of animal skins and feathers, we are calling upon the earth's magic and power to help us and heal us. The drum is the earth's heartbeat. When we dance in time to it, we are in sync with the earth and its marvelous rhythms. And when we perform the *Wacipi* in a circle, we are honoring the ancient miraculous circle of life. The circle of birth, childhood, adulthood, marriage, bravery, grief, and death.

One of the dances I perform and teach is called the hoop dance. I open my arms wide in the dance, like an eagle's wings, with the hoops spread out along them. That's what our life is like. We are connected to everything else. We are woven into the sacred hoops. And that is the beauty of the powwow.

The *Tioyspaye* ("extended family") invites you to the powwow. Sit down and watch the mysterious spectacle. Or stand around the drum and listen. Or join us in an intertribal dance. If you don't mind a little dust and heat (if it's outdoors and it's summer), you will leave feeling refreshed and happy.

Neta kola ("Your friend"),
D. Chief Eagle, Jr.
Rosebud Sioux Hoopdancer
Director, Hoop Dance Academy

According to some of the oldest stories told on this land, the first dancers were the animals. This was a long time ago, before books and television. Back then, buffalo danced in huge herds, slowly moving their heads from side to side. Deer danced with leaping strides. Fish danced in the rivers, reflecting sunlight. Whooping cranes faced each other and spread their wings wide, turning in circles, while woodpeckers beat a hollow tree for a drum.

Some stories say it was the animals who taught people how to dance. They taught people which dances brought luck in hunting, which cured illness, and which brought visions. Dancing was a way of expressing friendships with all the other creatures that shared the earth.

Whether animals still dance or not, most people don't know. You have to watch an animal a long time before you can say for sure. You have to understand how it thinks and how it knows the land. You have to dance in its skin and feel in your muscles the same movements that the animal feels. Most of us don't have reason to do that anymore. We live in an age in which the wisdom of animals is ignored.

But there are still celebrations all across America in which the old dances—the first dances—are performed. The dancers are the first people of America, the Native Americans, and the celebrations are called powwows. When the dancers put on their outfits of buckskin and feathers, they reach out to their ancestors—to the "ones who have gone before." They come as close as anyone can to that ancient way of living. They step lightly. They lift their eagle staffs in praise. Dancing in a circle, they complete the sacred circle of life.

Left: This traditional dancer honors the spirit of an animal by wearing a coyote mask over his head.

Louis is a Native American boy who lives on the Flathead Reservation in Montana. A member of the Pend Oreille tribe, he became a dancer when he was only four years old. Now, at nine, he's big enough to be a valuable third baseman for his Little League baseball team. In the winter, after school, he practices hook shots for his basketball team in the gym. But dancing is the passion that goes deepest with him. "I almost can't remember a time when I wasn't a dancer," he says.

Right, far right: Louis's grandfather, Pat, is an elder on the Flathead Reservation in Montana. He has danced since he was a young man.

Louis mostly learned how to dance from his grandfather, Pat. Pat works with the tribal health department as the director of the Elders Assistance Program. He is also in charge of arranging the reservation's dance events. Pat has been a dancer for most of his life.

There was a time, earlier this century, when most Native American dances were banned. The Indian people had fallen victim to the great wave of American settlement. Professional hunters had killed off the huge animal herds that the Indians relied on not only for food but also as examples of how to live as a society on the earth. Many Indian villages were burned to the ground, and their crops were destroyed. The people were forced to give up the great, bountiful land that was their home for much smaller reservations, where the soil was often too poor for crops. In order to survive, many Native Americans had to depend on handouts from the government.

The government of the United States believed that the best way to help the Indians was to force a new way of life on them. Government officials encouraged Indians to fence their lands and raise animals and crops for money—notions that were foreign to them. Government regulations required children to be removed from their families and villages and sent far away to live in Indian schools, where they were not allowed to speak their native languages. Officials discouraged everything that tied Native Americans to their past, including dance.

"Those were some bad times," says Pat, shaking his head. "There weren't many jobs on the reservations, and there was a lot of hunger and illness. And when your culture is taken away like that, you lose your self-esteem."

Things have gradually gotten a little better on reservations. There are more jobs now, and better housing. And Indian people have assumed more control over their own affairs. Most importantly, Native Americans are taking renewed pride in their culture. Some people are learning the old languages. Some are writing down the old stories and myths. And more and more Indian people are performing the dances again.

"It makes you feel good to see so many people interested in dance now," says Pat. "Especially the kids. When you see kids out there dancing, you know your people will be strong for a long time."

Below: Louis learns new moves by watching videos made at powwows. Then he and his brother Michael practice at their grandfather's house.

Louis spends several hours a week practicing his dance moves. "Sometimes we learn by watching the videos we've made at dances," he says. "We've also got some music tapes of Indian singers that we listen to as we practice."

Louis practices at home, and when he learns a new move, he goes over to his grandfather's house to show him. They put on some music and, as Louis dances, Pat watches closely, humming along and tapping his knee to the rhythm of the song. Sometimes he offers advice to help Louis improve.

"The most important thing is to listen to the drum," says Pat. "The drum tells you how to dance. If the drum speeds up, you have to speed up. If it slows down, you have to slow down. On the strong, accented beats, you have to honor the drum by raising your staff or dipping low."

Louis lifts his feet in time to the music. He taps his left foot lightly, then firmly, and then his right foot lightly, then firmly. *Tap, STEP, tap, STEP, tap, STEP, tap, STEP . . .*

The drumbeat is steady, and the singers' voices are high and piercing. Louis recognizes the song on the tape. There's a good chance he knows the singers, too. It may be the Black Lodge Singers from the Blackfoot tribe. Or maybe the Pistol Creek Singers from his own reservation. That music is happiness, as sweet as a spring breeze. Louis whirls and dips, sashays to the side, backsteps, crosses his legs, and spins.

"Bend low," Pat says. "Keep your head up. Good!"

Sometimes his brother Michael and his Uncle David join in. Michael is a year older than Louis, and David is eight years older. They have all been doing traditional dances for years.

Like other traditional dancers, they wear outfits that look like the outfits of the old days—the days before Columbus. They hold staffs or bird-wing fans, and their outfits are made out of animal skins and feathers. They move like hunters stalking their prey or warriors sneaking up on the enemy.

But this year Louis wants to try a different kind of dance, called the grass dance. Recently it has become very popular among Native Americans, though it has been around for a long time. Grass dancers wear colorful outfits with long strings of wool hanging from the shoulders and trousers. The dance is more fluid than traditional dances. Some people say it started when men braided strands of sweet grass into their outfits when courting women. Others say the dance came in a vision to a holy man who was seeking a way to heal the illnesses of his people. Many things are unknown about these dances, since most began long before history was written down.

Right: Grass dance outfits were originally hung with braids of sweet grass. Now they are hung with colorful strands of wool.

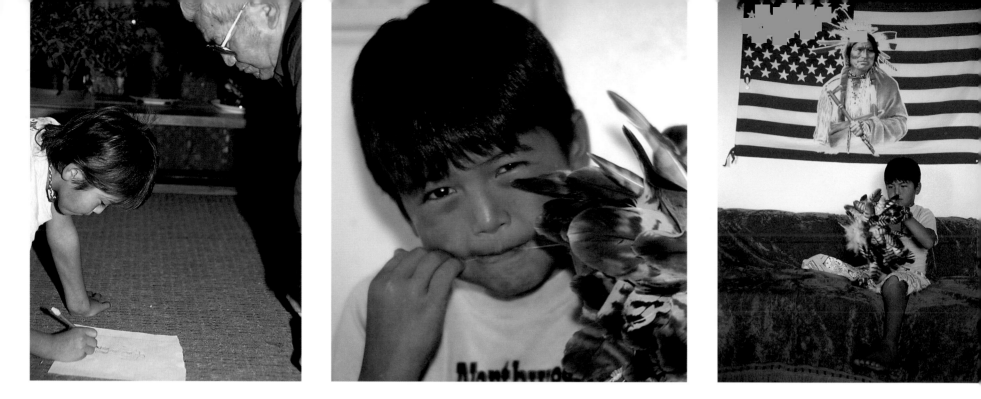

Before Louis can do the grass dance, though, he has to design his outfit. With his grandfather looking on, he draws a picture of what he wants a friend of the family to sew.

"I want mine to be like the flag," he says. "Red, white, and blue, with stars."

The design has a long tradition. In the previous centuries, U.S. flags were often given to Indian tribes as a sign of peace, and the Indians also took the flags from U.S. cavalry troops they had defeated in battles. Often the flags were the most colorful fabric the Indians owned, and eventually many of them were incorporated into Native American ceremonial dress.

Louis makes some parts of his outfit by himself. He makes a feather cap by sewing feathers onto a baseball cap so that none

Above: Louis gets help in designing and making his grass dance outfit from his grandfather and mother.

of the fabric shows. He makes a staff by attaching a deer antler to a stick and wrapping it in cloth. And with help from his uncles and aunts, he makes his own moccasins and a bustle of eagle feathers to be tied at his back.

The most valuable thing a dancer can add to an outfit is an eagle feather. For many tribes the eagle is the most sacred animal. Watching an eagle soar with its white head gleaming and its wings spread wide, the dancer can't help but feel blessed. They are beautiful, noble birds. But now, unfortunately, bald eagles have been shot and poisoned almost to extinction. In order to save them, laws were passed that make it illegal to hunt or trap eagles for any purpose. However, the U.S. Fish and Wildlife Service realized the religious value of eagle feathers for Native American people and made a special arrangement for them. Now whenever a dead eagle is found, it is sent to Portland, Oregon, where it is kept frozen in a locker. To get eagle feathers for his grandson's outfits, Pat has to sign a paper, and then the government mails the eagle feathers to him on the reservation.

Louis attaches the feathers to his outfit with great care. He is careful not to let an eagle feather get dirty, and he tries never to let one touch the ground. That would be disrespectful. And disrespect brings bad luck.

This is part of what Louis learns from his grandfather. Respect for the eagle. Respect for the ways of his ancestors. After sewing each eagle feather onto the baseball cap, Louis straightens and grooms it, just as the eagle did when it was alive.

Above: Louis wears his new grass dance outfit.

Louis and his family attend between fifteen and twenty powwows a year. They often just drive down the road to dance inside the community center in the town of St. Ignatius, Montana, or to the bigger powwow grounds in the town of Arlee. But sometimes they travel as far as three hundred miles to the reservation of another tribe. The dances they participate in are part of the northern powwow circuit, which includes most of the northern Great Plains. The southern circuit is centered in Oklahoma. Some of the tribes that host the powwows have different dances and customs, but there are still a lot of similarities. And even though some dancers may be far from home when visiting a different reservation, they're always treated like friends.

While traveling to a powwow, David puts on a tape of Indian singers. "I used to listen to rock 'n' roll, like most of the kids in my high school," he says. "But recently all I've been listening to are powwow songs."

It's about the only music that Louis listens to, also. "I sing the songs to myself sometimes when I'm walking to school," he says, "or when I'm waiting for a ball to come my way at third base, you know, during a Little League game."

Louis, Michael, and David sing along with the tape as they drive through the countryside—"singing Indian," they call it. Pat hums along, tapping his hand on the steering wheel in time to the music. Most of the songs don't have any words. They're just syllables, like *hey, ya, ha, ha, hey. . . .* The syllables keep the rhythm, while the melody lifts and falls like a hawk soaring on a wind.

Below: This is the original Montana homeland of Louis's tribe . . .
far right: a place where beauty walks freely.

They drive through forests and across high dusty plains,
past cattle ranches and fields of wheat. This is the country that
their people used to wander through in search of buffalo. It is
where their ancestors are buried. Big rivers wind through the
valleys. High mountains rise in the distance. In the afternoon
the sky darkens with black clouds, and soon it is raining—a
brief summer thunderstorm. The windshield wipers seem to
keep time to the songs on the tape.

Right: You always dance best, says Pat, when you dance for others.

Before reaching the powwow, Pat usually gives the boys a little talk. "When you're out there dancing this weekend," he says, "remember that you're not just dancing to win a contest. There are more important reasons to dance. You should pick out someone not as fortunate as you are, and keep them in mind when you're dancing—an elder who is too old to dance or someone who's sick or someone who has lost a loved one. If you remember to do that, your dancing will be good."

The boys nod. They know what Pat is talking about. The dance arbor (the ring in the middle of a powwow where all the dancing is done) is a special place. When you're dancing in the circle of the dance arbor, whatever good thoughts you have usually come back to you.

Louis has a friend who once learned that lesson in an unforgettable way. Arriving at a powwow one day, the dancer saw an old man sitting near the entrance, with a cane in his hand and his head hanging down. The dancer thought he looked like the saddest person he'd ever seen. He waved and said, "How ya doin'?"

But the old man didn't even look up. "Not so good," he mumbled. "My legs are bad, and my dancin' days are long gone."

The dancer paused and then reached out his hand. "I'm going to be dancing for you tonight, old man," he said. The man raised his eyes and weakly shook the dancer's hand.

According to Louis's friend, that was the best night of dancing he ever had. He felt the singing and the drumming inside his body as he danced, and the colors of his feathers and fringe shivered in the lights. The earth felt good beneath his feet. The great sky full of stars wheeled overhead. And every now and then, he saw the old man sitting in the stands, watching him intensely.

When the dancing was over for the night, he walked back to his pup tent and fell into an exhausted sleep. In the morning he was suddenly awakened by someone shaking the tent. He opened the flap and looked out. It was an old woman, and she was holding out a big breakfast of eggs and toast and coffee.

"I'm the wife of the man you danced for last night," she said. "He wanted you to know that he woke up this morning feeling happier than he has in years. So we made you this breakfast. Thanks!"

Powwows usually last a whole weekend, and if it's a holiday weekend, the dancing, singing, and drumming go on from Friday night through Monday morning. So the first thing Louis and his family do after arriving at the powwow site is set up their campsite in the encampment.

"My grandpa has a camper on his truck," says Louis, "and sometimes we sleep in that. But if the whole family comes— all my brothers and sisters and cousins and aunts and uncles—we also have to bring along tents and sleeping bags."

An encampment is like a small city. There are trailers, tipis, motor homes, vans, pup tents, food stands, portable outhouses, showers, arts-and-crafts stalls, a first-aid station, and even a small police department. At some powwows the tipis are given the place of honor in the center of the encampment, and there you can see tipi after tipi with their wooden poles sticking through their peaks. Their sides are often painted with designs—buffalo skulls or bears or beautiful geometrical shapes—some of them handed down from ancient ancestors.

Top: Almost overnight, a small village pops up around the powwow grounds, with tipis . . .
middle: stalls for food vendors . . .
bottom: and stalls for sellers of beads, which the dancers use to decorate their outfits.

After their camp is set up, Louis and Michael stroll around the powwow grounds. They watch a family raise the poles of their tipi and then enclose the frame with canvas. A young boy trots by on a horse, and Louis notices that both the boy and the horse are wearing bright yellow face paint. Nearby, a woman shows off her new baby, sleeping in her beaded cradleboard, to a group of friends. All around them the dancers are getting their outfits ready—smoothing the feathers, straightening the leather fringe, weaving strips of weasel fur into their braids, painting their faces. Somewhere in the distance, a drum starts to pound, and Louis taps his feet and dips and twirls. An old man laughs and waves at them—a friend they made at another powwow, another year.

Cars are still arriving, and the encampment keeps getting bigger. Some powwows involve as many as fifteen hundred dancers, with many more friends and family members along to enjoy the festivities. Where do all the people come from? At the powwows Louis goes to, the license plates say Montana, Idaho, Washington, Oregon, Wyoming, Nevada, South Dakota, even Canada. But as the drum pounds louder, and as more and more dancers appear in their outfits, Louis knows that where they come from is older than any state or country. They come from tribes: Lakota, Blackfoot, Salish, Nez Perce, Chippewa, Ponca, Crow, Shoshone, Cheyenne, Apache, Navajo, Cherokee. . . .

"A powwow is a celebration of being Indian," says Louis. "It's a way of seeing our friends, and keeping up our traditions, too."

Above top: A dancer preens his feathers before the powwow begins.
Above bottom: Many of the designs seen at a powwow are the same as those used hundreds of years ago.

23

The boys pay a dancer's fee at the registration booth and receive the contest number tags to pin on their outfits. Then they walk around the dance arbor to watch the drum groups as they set up their drums and adjust the microphones. When the master of ceremonies announces over the loudspeakers that the Grand Entry is in half an hour, Louis and Michael return to their camp to get ready.

David and Pat are already in their traditional dance outfits by the time Louis and Michael get back. Louis helps David straighten the feathers on his bustle, then gets into his own outfit. Louis decides that first he'll dance traditional, and then later on switch to his woolen grass dance outfit. He tries out a few steps while singing a song. Then they all head toward the arbor to join the line of dancers waiting for the Grand Entry.

It is late afternoon now, and the sun is low in the sky. The dancers are lined up at the east end of the arbor. The spectators are sitting in the grass or on the bleachers. The arbor is empty. The drums are quiet.

"Let's have a good song from the host drum," says the MC over the loudspeakers.

A drum begins pounding, and then one strong, high voice lifts above the steady beat. A moment later the other singers join in, and now all the dancers are moving their feet in time to the drum, their ankle bells chiming. The feeling is electric. The urge toward movement and celebration is irresistible.

Left top: In the back of the family pickup, Louis gathers together his outfit.
Left bottom: Making the final adjustments to his outfit, Louis looks in the rearview mirror of the family camper.

Left: Lining up for the Grand Entry, the youngest dancers go toward the rear . . .
below: with the tiny tots bringing up the end.

"This is one of the most exciting moments of the pow-wow," says Louis. "During the Grand Entry, the dancers enter the arbor one by one. The people carrying the flags and eagle staff go first, followed by the men dancers, then the women dancers, and then us kids. The tiny tots go last."

From his position near the end of the line, Louis watches as the dancers file into the arbor. The line passes close to the spectators, and once a complete circle is made, the leader moves inward to make room for more dancers.

By the time Louis enters the arbor, the dance has formed a great spiral.

"Ah ho!" shouts the announcer over the drumming and singing. "Welcome to the powwow! This is how Indian people celebrate their culture! This is how we honor our traditions! The powwow has been practiced on this continent for more than ten thousand years. Some of the dances you'll see here this weekend are more than thirty times older than the United States. May we keep on dancing for as many years in the future!"

The lead drummer hits a few strong, accented beats, and the dancers raise their staffs in response. The men's feather bustles tremble. The women's shawls fly. Thousands of feet are stepping in unison on the earth!

Below: Louis and the other dancers spin and spiral into the dance arbor during the Grand Entry—a moment of intense excitement and enthusiasm.

The song comes to an end after the arbor is full, and a respectful silence falls over the crowd as the eagle staff and the U.S. and Canadian flags are presented. A short speech is given, and then a prayer. Finally, the flag song—an Indian anthem—is sung by a drum group.

Because Pat is one of the leaders of the tribe, he is often asked to offer the opening speech and prayer. He begins by welcoming everyone to the powwow, and he urges the dancers to give their best effort in their dances. "But remember, too, what a powwow is all about," he adds. "Don't think too much about that contest money. That'll only get in the way of you and the drum. We're here to celebrate our traditions. We're here to keep the sacred circle of our nations and families complete."

Then he shuts his eyes and raises his eagle staff to the sky. The prayer he offers is in his native Pend Oreille language, and the words are rich and rhythmical. It's a language he uses for special occasions. He is one of the last few people to speak it.

The first dances at a powwow are usually the intertribal dances. Anyone can join in an intertribal. It is a time for people to get up and circle around the arbor together. Some people do their special dances—like the grass dance or a traditional dance. Others just walk around with their friends, talking while doing a relaxed *tap, step*. You can also see several new parents—or new grandparents—dancing around with babies in their arms. One is never too young to start on the powwow circuit!

Above: Louis's grandfather recites the prayer in his native language.

Above: A common sight at a powwow: mallets resting on a drum while drummers await their turn to perform.

As each new dance begins, a different song is sung by a different drum. Often there are as many as ten drum groups at a powwow, and at the dances Louis goes to, they are all spread out around the edge of the arbor. They are named for the family that owns the drum, or the place or tribe the drum group comes from, or for a symbol meaningful to the Indian people.

These are some of their names: Kicking Woman, Two Rivers, Little Falls, Crowshoe, Red Wolf, Pistol Creek, Black Lodge, Stoney Park, Blackfoot Crossing, Morning Star, Young Grey Horse, Teton Travelers, Eagle Whistles, Chief Cliff, Chiniki Lake, Eagleman, Badlands, Youngbloods. . . .

Some of the drums at a powwow are store-bought bass drums—the same type a marching band uses in a parade. Others are more traditional. They are made by hand out of hollow tree trunks, with elk or moose skins stretched across the tops and bottoms. The mallets are wooden sticks with their ends wrapped in the skin of a deer. As the drummers set up the drums before the powwow, they hang eagle feathers from their sides. They also spread an offering of tobacco across the tops of the drums and rub it in. Sometimes the drummers purify the area with smudging ceremonies, waving the smoke from a burning braid of sweet grass around the drum.

A drum is made of earth, of living things. Its shape is round, too. Round like the dance arbor. Like the floor of a tipi. Like the sun and the moon. Like the sacred circle of family, friends, and tribe.

"The sound of a drum," says Pat, "is really the sound of the earth's heartbeat."

That beat is rich and low and steady. At the beginning of a song, it sets the rhythm by itself, without any voices accompanying it. And then one of the drummers starts singing the first verse. He squeezes his eyes shut with concentration, seeming to call up the song from deep inside. His voice is high and clear and full of trills, yet piercing and loud.

A moment later the rest of the singers join in. They sing at the tops of their lungs. They sound like an entire nation.

Often the drum speeds up in the middle of the song. Listening carefully, the dancers pick up their pace. And then the drum goes faster. Pretty soon the drumbeat pushes all other thoughts aside. All the dancers can do is listen and dance; all the drum group can do is drum and sing. There's no room to think about anything else.

"It's hard to describe the feeling," says Louis. "When you've got a good drum and your dancing is good, it's like the earth is helping you dance."

The music, which has its own definite structure and patterns of repetition, evolved in a world very different from the one we know. It comes from a time when the forests stood unbroken and the virgin prairies stretched to the horizon, when the eagle was not an endangered species. The songs echo that time. When they are sung, animals and people are related again.

Right: The Kicking Woman family of the Blackfoot tribe is a well-known drum group in the northern powwow circuit.

Louis and the other powwow dancers stay up late into the night before returning to their camps, and then the next day, around noon, it all begins again. The drums take up the beat once more, and the dancers put on their outfits. The announcer jokes with the crowd. Volunteers sell raffle tickets to raise money for dance contests. Giveaways take place, in which one person or a family honors another by offering gifts of food and blankets. Under a roof in the middle of the encampment, people are playing stick games—an ancient form of gambling that involves singing and beating small hand drums. Some powwows also put on rodeos and parades. Big feasts may be given. Horse races are held, and footraces for the kids.

There is time for a few more intertribal dances, mixed with team dances, in which three dancers perform together, or round dances, in which two lines of people pass each other by and shake hands. In an owl dance, men and women dance cheek to cheek. In a hoop dance, a single dancer dances with many hoops linked together along his arms like giant wings.

Top: Some powwows include parades . . . *middle:* horse races . . . *bottom:* and special dances, such as the hoop dance.
Right: In an honor dance, everyone dances behind the person being honored.
Far right: After a few dances in the hot sun, a little refreshment tastes great!

During the heat of the day, Louis sometimes takes a break to cool off with an icy drink. He also takes time to study the other dancers. "I think that's a good way to learn how to dance," he says. "You watch the other dancers, and then try out their moves at home."

Occasionally an honor dance is given for certain people or families. Today it is the oldest war veteran on the reservation who is being honored. When he was young, he fought in World War I. Now he is old and confined to a wheelchair. A short speech is made by one of the tribal leaders, and then his family and close friends wheel him around the arbor. A long line of dancers follows behind as a drum group sings a slow song.

Below: Jingle dresses are hung with cones made from the tin lids of chewing tobacco cans.

Soon it's time for the contest dances to begin. This is when the dancers put on their best show. The MC announces the dance, and the judges position themselves at different spots inside the arbor.

Women's contests are usually held before men's, and in the powwows that Louis and his grandfather go to, the jingle dancers go first. They walk into the arbor with a distinctive clatter.

"You see those cones on their dresses?" Louis points out. "They're all made from the tin lids of Copenhagen chewing tobacco cans. The dancers buy them directly from the company, and then twist them into little cones, which they sew onto their dresses."

When the music begins, the dancers start dancing. A jingle dance song has a quick beat, and the cones clatter right along with the drums. Because the dresses are tight-fitting, the dancers have to move up and down a lot, instead of sideways, and this makes the cones jingle all the more.

"Back in the old days," says Pat, "no one even heard of the jingle dance. Now, all of a sudden, it's real popular. I even have two granddaughters who are jingle dancers."

When the dance is done, the contestants remain in the arbor awhile longer while the judges write down a few more notes and figure out how many points to give the dancers. Judges not only watch to see how well the dancers perform, but they also give extra points for a good outfit.

Above: When a jingle dancer dances, the metal cones clatter together.

The next dance is the women's fancy dance, also called the shawl dance.

"This is a real fast one," says Louis. "Sometimes when the dancers spin with their shawls, they look like they're going to start flying."

This dance has become popular recently, too. In fact, participation by women in powwows is a new development. In the old days, women could most often be seen standing behind a drum, singing along, in high, clear voices. But now women are involved in every aspect of the powwow. There are women drummers and women judges and women who carry the flags during the Grand Entry.

The women fancy dancers spin and leap. Their dresses bell out as they spin, and their colorful, embroidered shawls flutter like wings. When ten or so shawl dancers are spinning around each other out in the arbor, it often looks as though someone has let loose a flock of wild birds.

The one dance that women have performed for a long time is called the women's traditional. It is usually the last women's dance to be performed. The outfits are made out of buckskin that is sometimes dyed with deep, rich colors and adorned with beadwork, shells, feathers, or even elk teeth. From the dancers' arms a buckskin fringe hangs down almost to the floor. The dance is very slow and stately. The women take light, little steps—the smallest of *tap, steps*—and hold their heads steady and straight. They fan themselves with their feather fans, and as they dance the fringe sways back and forth. The judges look not only at the women's dresses

Left top: The women's fancy dance, or shawl dance, is a high-speed blur of color.
Left bottom: The women's traditional dance is slow-paced and elegant.

and the way they carry themselves, but also at the movement of the fringe. With the best traditional dancers, the fringe sways as though blown by a gentle breeze.

It is late afternoon now, and a quiet settles over the dance arbor as everyone breaks for dinner. The dancers wander back to their camps, their ankle bells ringing. They take off their feather caps and eagle bustles. They lean their eagle staffs against their cars. They sprawl on lawn chairs outside their tents, glad to get off their feet for a while.

Louis pauses at a refreshment stand to read aloud the food list. "Hamburgers, hot dogs, corn dogs, Indian tacos, fry bread, ice cream, soda pop, snow cones . . . pretty much the same food you can get at any fair," he says.

Louis knows his mother is making sandwiches for her hungry dancers, so he finally settles on a soda pop and then hurries along.

Right: Grass dancers stroll among the concessions during a late-afternoon break.

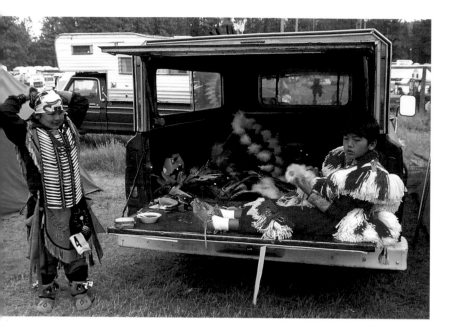

Above: Louis and Michael take a well-deserved rest during the late-afternoon dinner break.

Back at camp Louis's grandfather is hanging his eagle bustle on the door of the truck, making sure the feathers don't touch the ground. He removes his headdress, straightens some of the feathers, and sets it down on the bed of the truck.

"It's not a real old outfit," he says. "I've only had it for twenty years or so. Once I had one that was much older than that," he says. "It was handed down to me from my father, who got it from his father, and so on. No one really knew how old it was. Maybe it was around when Lewis and Clark came through!"

Pat takes a bite of his sandwich and ponders the thought for a while.

"But then, sometime back in the 1950s, it was stolen," he says. "I had hung it up in a tipi at a powwow and just stepped out for a while. When I came back, it was gone. It hit me pretty hard. You can't put a price on those things, you know. I didn't dance for the next thirteen years after that."

He shakes his head slowly. "Whenever I'm in Seattle or Portland," he adds, "I always visit the museums to see if it turned up there, but I have never found it."

Because the judges of the contest dances give extra points for a good outfit, the best dancers care as much for their outfits as they do for the dance itself. They labor for hours and hours on the design, the intricate beadwork, the arrangement of the feathers, the flow of the fringe. They keep their eyes open for any item that might contribute to the outfit, like an old medallion or an armband. In the end a powwow outfit may be worth thousands of dollars.

Some people say that recently powwows have been getting too commercial. They worry that all the dancers care about is winning the contests and getting the money. They point out that in the past there were never dancers, as there are now, who made a living going from powwow to powwow and competing for the big prizes.

But others say that the contests and the prize money actually encourage a respect for the old traditions. A dancer can't win a dance without a top-notch outfit. And to make a good outfit requires a great respect for the traditions.

While everyone is still eating, Louis pulls out a suitcase from the back of the truck. He disappears into a tent for a while and when he finally comes back out, he's wearing his new grass dance outfit.

He sits on the back of the truck and pulls on his moccasins. Next, he straps two large sets of bells to his ankles, then straightens out the wool fringe on the outfit.

By the time he's done, the powwow drums are pounding again. The MC is calling the dancers to the arbor. It's time for the men's competitions!

Right: Louis straps a set of bells around his ankles.

Above: Though the men's fancy dance is the most energetic of the dances, there is nothing "wild" or careless about it. The dancers are highly disciplined performers who studiously practice their moves.

When the men fancy dancers compete, it's easy to imagine that a troupe of spirits has taken over the dance arbor. Their outfits are shiny and bright, with fringe and feathers flowing everywhere. They wear two big bustles of feathers on their backs, one at the waist, and another at the shoulders. They wear colorful crests of porcupine hairs (called roaches) on their heads, with a pair of eagle feathers standing straight up above the roaches. Some fancy dancers attach metallic ribbons to the tips of their feather bustles. If they happen to be dancing at night, under the spotlights, the dancers look like flames floating around the arbor, and the metallic ribbons follow them like a stream of sparks.

Fancy dancers move all over the arbor when they dance. They step high, quickly turning one way while their fringe and ribbons are still going the other. They spin and turn and leap. Some even do handsprings or flips. The fancy dance grew out of the grass dance, and the two still share some of the same moves. But the fancy dance is much faster. It requires more energy than any other dance on the powwow circuit.

When the song is over, the dancers are exhausted. They pant and sag, and beads of sweat appear on their faces. They look as though they can barely stand. But the MC asks the crowd if they want to see another dance, and everyone cheers.

"Give us rousing song, Eagle Drum," commands the MC.

And so the beat begins again. The fierce, quavering voices start up, and the fancy dancers go at it once more, leaping and spinning and flashing around the arbor. It's no wonder that the best dancers keep in shape by jogging and other exercise.

When the contest for the men's traditional dance is called, Louis's brother Michael, his Uncle David, and his grandfather find their places in the arbor. This is their dance, the one they have been practicing all year.

When the drum begins to beat, the dancers step in time with their feet, bending at the waist. They bob their heads and look from side to side. The movement imitates the stalking of a hunter as he searches for prey and looks for tracks, keeping a wary eye out for enemies.

Some of the traditional dancers wear face paint. One wears a coyote mask, and when he bends his head down, it looks as though Coyote himself has joined the dance. Others might wear buffalo horns on their heads or fox pelts over their backs. The dancers all carry staffs with eagle talons or antlers attached to the tops. When a drummer hits an accent beat on the drum, they raise the staffs high in the air. Traditional dancers don't spin or move as fast as the fancy dancers. But they still need a lot of stamina and strength to carry that heavy weight of feathers, buckskin, and bells.

The drum plays on, and the singers' voices ring out. The dancers step quickly as the music speeds up. Their ankle bells chime, and yet they set their moccasined feet down so lightly they seem to float. They turn in a small circle, holding their staffs level to the ground, then raising them high, then dipping low again, almost touching their elbows to the ground. When they sense that the song is nearing its end, they throw in a few more dazzling moves before freezing motionless with the last beat.

Above top: Face paint expresses the individuality of the dancer.
Above bottom: When this traditional dancer dips his head, the spirit of Coyote joins the dance.

Right: A powwow is a mix of color, movement, and good feelings.

Before Louis dances, a few more intertribal dances take place. It has been a good celebration, and everyone is in fine spirits. The crowd gets bigger around the drum, and everybody sings. Another drum takes up the next song, and the dancers follow without losing a beat. Many new friends have been made, and old friendships renewed. "You can't help but feel good about everybody out there," says Pat, "after you've all been in the dance arbor together, moving in time to the drumbeat."

"After a whole weekend of this," adds David, "you begin to think that dancing is your life."

But then something happens that suddenly makes everyone turn serious. During one of the intertribal dances, an eagle feather falls from someone's outfit. It doesn't take long for other dancers to see it lying on the ground, and a few of them, still dancing, form a ring around it to protect it. When the songs ends, someone tells the MC about it and he tells the crowd that an eagle feather has fallen on the ground.

"Please bear with us while we honor the feather in the Indian way," he says over the loudspeakers. "To us, the eagle is the most sacred of animals. It represents wisdom and knowledge. It soars above the world, looking down on us with powerful eyes, and where it flies the earth is blessed. This is why we wear its feathers on our outfits. We hope that some of its wisdom will be granted to us. So when an eagle feather falls to the ground, it's not a good sign. For one thing, it means we haven't made our outfits carefully enough, which can happen if we don't treat our culture with respect. Mistakes can happen, of course, but they have to be corrected. So can we please all stand while one of the elders picks up the fallen feather?"

Suddenly there is absolute silence as an old man enters the arbor and walks toward the fallen feather. He passes a feather fan over the fallen feather a few times, and then he gently lifts the feather onto a tray. At some powwows a special "fallen article" dance is performed, in which some of the elders dance around the feather in the direction opposite to the one the dances had been going. But whatever action is taken with a fallen eagle feather, the ceremony is sacred. No photographs are allowed. The drums, which have been beating almost continuously since the powwow began, are silent. The audience stands, and the dancers look on quietly.

When the elder has removed the feather, the MC thanks the crowd for their courtesy and respect, and then the powwow continues.

Above: Pat makes one last adjustment to Louis's outfit before the grass dance competition.

Before the grass competition is called, Louis checks one last time to make sure his outfit is on right. He tightens the straps and adjusts the fringe, and his grandfather helps him straighten his roach. Louis dances in places a little, to get warmed up.

"Let's get the grass dancers out into the arbor and see what they can do!" announces the MC.

Louis walks into the arbor with the other grass dancers and then waits for the music to begin. Though a couple hundred people are watching him, he doesn't really feel nervous.

"When all your friends and family are dancers, there's not much to be nervous about," he says. "It's just something that's a part of life, not separated from it."

The drums begin, and Louis immediately picks up the rhythm with his feet. He lifts them high and turns gracefully, steps wide, turns again, makes a small leap, and turns the other way. Out of the corner of his eye, he sees the other grass dancers spinning beside him. He sees his grandfather watching him proudly, and his brothers, and all the people of his tribe and the other tribes. He sees the clouds turning in the sky and the grass blurring beneath him.

Louis moves smoothly from step to step. The wool fringe on his outfit flows. His roach sways. His ankle bells ring. Listening carefully, he picks up his pace as the drum speeds up. As Louis spins, everything blurs into motion.

Above: As he performs the grass dance, the woolen strands on Louis's outfit sway like the grass of a prairie.

There is the strange and wonderful feeling that a powwow creates. The music came out of the land, and the dancing renews the old kinship. The trees sway in the wind. A pair of hawks circle in the sky. The distant hills catch the orange glow of the late sun. Louis glides like a river as he dances. Each move is different; each adds to the beauty.

"Ah ho!" shouts the MC when the drum finally quits beating and Louis and the other dancers come to a stop. "Let's hear it for these grass dancers!"

While the powwow officials are tallying the judges' points and dividing up the contest money, there is time for a few more intertribal dances. Louis sits down at a drum where his friends are singing. He takes up a mallet and joins in on a song. The stars are out now. The moon sits high in the sky.

Finally the MC announces that the judges' points have been tallied. The crowd gathers around as the names of the winners and runners-up are called for each dance and age category. At some powwows a good dancer can make a lot of money. But for young dancers, the prize money is a modest recognition of their talents and hard work, and it encourages them to keep at it.

In the young boys' category for grass dancing, Louis takes second place. He walks out into the arbor to accept the envelope with ten dollars in it and then shakes hands with the officials, including his grandfather, who stands at the end of the line.

"This is great!" says Louis. "I've been saving up to buy some more beadwork for my outfit, and now I've got just enough money for it."

Above top: Part sacred and part social, a powwow brings together good friends.
Above bottom: Pat looks on with pride as Louis accepts his award.

Since it's too late to travel all the way home, Louis's family stays one last night at the encampment. In the morning they'll fold up the tents and say good-bye to their friends. Most of them they'll see in another couple weeks or so at the next powwow. Until then Louis will pass the time with school and homework, basketball or baseball, and practicing his dance moves.

But for now Louis lies in his sleeping bag, listening to the crickets chirping all around the tent. The drums are quiet, though after three days of dancing, he'll keep on hearing them for a while inside his head. His body is worn-out with the best kind of exhaustion—the kind that comes from grass dancing. From moving in step with his ancestors. On the powwow trail . . .

Somewhere a coyote's voice rises in the night, and another coyote calls in response, and then another somewhere far away. The drums beating in Louis's head, on the edge of sleep, match the rhythm of the crickets.

Somewhere a salmon shivers with its entire body as it leaps and falls, and an eagle dives for it, its feathers fluttering. An old elk, one of the elders, walks through the forest with its huge rack of antlers. Its hooves on the ground pound out a deep heartbeat. Behind Louis's closed eyes, a long line of dancers, stretching back in time, raise their staffs in praise.

"In the dance arbor," says Louis's grandfather, "you are at the middle of the world."

This is a partial listing of the hundreds of powwows that take place around the United States and Canada every year. Major powwows are usually held annually on the same weekend. Call the local tribal headquarters for more information.

Globe, **Ariz.**: *Apache Days*   Labor Day Weekend
Window Rock, **Ariz.**: *Navajo Nation Fair*   Labor Day Weekend
Berkeley, **Calif.**: *University of California, Berkeley, Powwow*   Third Weekend of April
Fresno, **Calif.**: *Tewaquachi Powwow*   Third Weekend of April
Long Beach, **Calif.**: *Red Nations Celebration*   Fourth Weekend of May
Brocket, **Alberta, Canada**: *Annual Piegan Indian Days*   First Weekend of August
Calgary, **Alberta, Canada**: *Sarcee Powwow & Rodeo*   Last Weekend of July
Ignacio, **Colo.**: *Southern Ute Tribal Fair & Powwow*   Second Weekend of September
Hollywood, **Fla.**: *Seminole Tribal Fair & Rodeo*   Second Weekend of February
St. George, **Ga.**: *Cherokees of Georgia Powwow*   First Weekend of October
Fort Hall, **Idaho**: *Shoshone Bannock Festival & Rodeo*   Second Weekend of August
Lapwai, **Idaho**: *Chief Joseph & Warriors Memorial Powwow*   Third Weekend of June
Horton, **Kans.**: *Kickapoo Tribe in Kansas Annual Powwow*   Third Weekend of July
Hopkinsville, **Ky.**: *Trail of Tears Intertribal Powwow*   First Weekend of September
Old Town, **Maine**: *Indian Day, Indian Island*   August
Camp Rotary, **Mich.**: *First Peoples Powwow*   Second Weekend of June
Cass Lake, **Minn.**: *Wee-Gitchie-Ne-E-Dim Powwow*   Labor Day Weekend
Arlee, **Mont.**: *Arlee Powwow & Celebration*   First Week of July
Browning, **Mont.**: *North American Indian Days*   Second Weekend of July
Crow Agency, **Mont.**: *Crow Fair & Rodeo*   Third Weekend of July
Maxton, **N.C.**: *Tuscarora Nation of North Carolina Powwow*   Second Weekend of May
Macy, **Nebr.**: *Omaha Memorial Day Celebration*   Fourth Weekend of May
Gallup, **N. Mex.**: *Annual Intertribal Indian Ceremonial*   Second Weekend of August
Howes Cave, **N.Y.**: *Iroquois Indian Festival*   Labor Day Weekend
Pawnee, **Okla.**: *Annual Pawnee Indian Homecoming & Powwow*   Last Weekend of June
Tahlequah, **Okla.**: *Annual Pawnee Indian Homecoming & Powwow*   Labor Day Weekend
Bandon, **Oreg.**: *Coquille Indian Tribe Powwow*   Last Weekend of June
Charlestown, **R.I.**: *Narragansett Indian Annual August Meeting*   Second Weekend of August
Pine Ridge, **S.D.**: *Oglala Nation Fair & Rodeo*   First Weekend of August
Rosebud, **S.D.**: *Annual Rosebud Fair & Powwow*   Third Weekend of August
Nashville, **Tenn.**: *Powwow & Fall Festival*   Third Weekend of October
Grand Prairie, **Tex.**: *Annual National Championship Powwow*   First Weekend after Labor Day
Fort Duchesne, **Utah**: *Annual Northern Ute Powwow & Rodeo*   First Weekend of July
Suquamish, **Wash.**: *Annual Chief Seattle Day*   Third Weekend of August
Wellpinit, **Wash.**: *Annual Spokane Tribal Fair & Rodeo*   Labor Day Weekend
Lac du Flambeau, **Wis.**: *Bear River Powwow*   Second Weekend of July
Oneida, **Wis.**: *Oneida Powwow*   Fourth of July Weekend
Fort Washakie, **Wyo.**: *Shoshone Indian Fair*   Labor Day Weekend